DC SUPER HEROES

BATMAN™

TALES OF THE BATCAVE

BATCAVE

HARLEY QUINN'S HAT TRICK

by
MICHAEL DAHL

illustrated by
LUCIANO VECCHIO

Batman created by
BOB KANE WITH BILL FINGER

STONE ARCH BOOKS
a capstone imprint

Published by Stone Arch Books in 2018
A Capstone Imprint
1710 Roe Crest Drive
North Mankato, Minnesota 56003
www.mycapstone.com

STAR39736

Library of Congress Cataloging-in-Publication Data is available on the Library of
Congress website.

ISBN: 978-1-4965-5983-8 (hardcover)
ISBN: 978-1-4965-5995-1 (paperback)
ISBN: 978-1-4965-6008-7 (eBook PDF)

Summary: Harley Quinn is on the loose with a scheme that leads Batman and Robin to
a giant top hat trap.

Editor: Christopher Harbo
Designer: Brann Garvey

Printed and bound in the USA.
010831S18

TABLE OF CONTENTS

This is the BATCAVE.

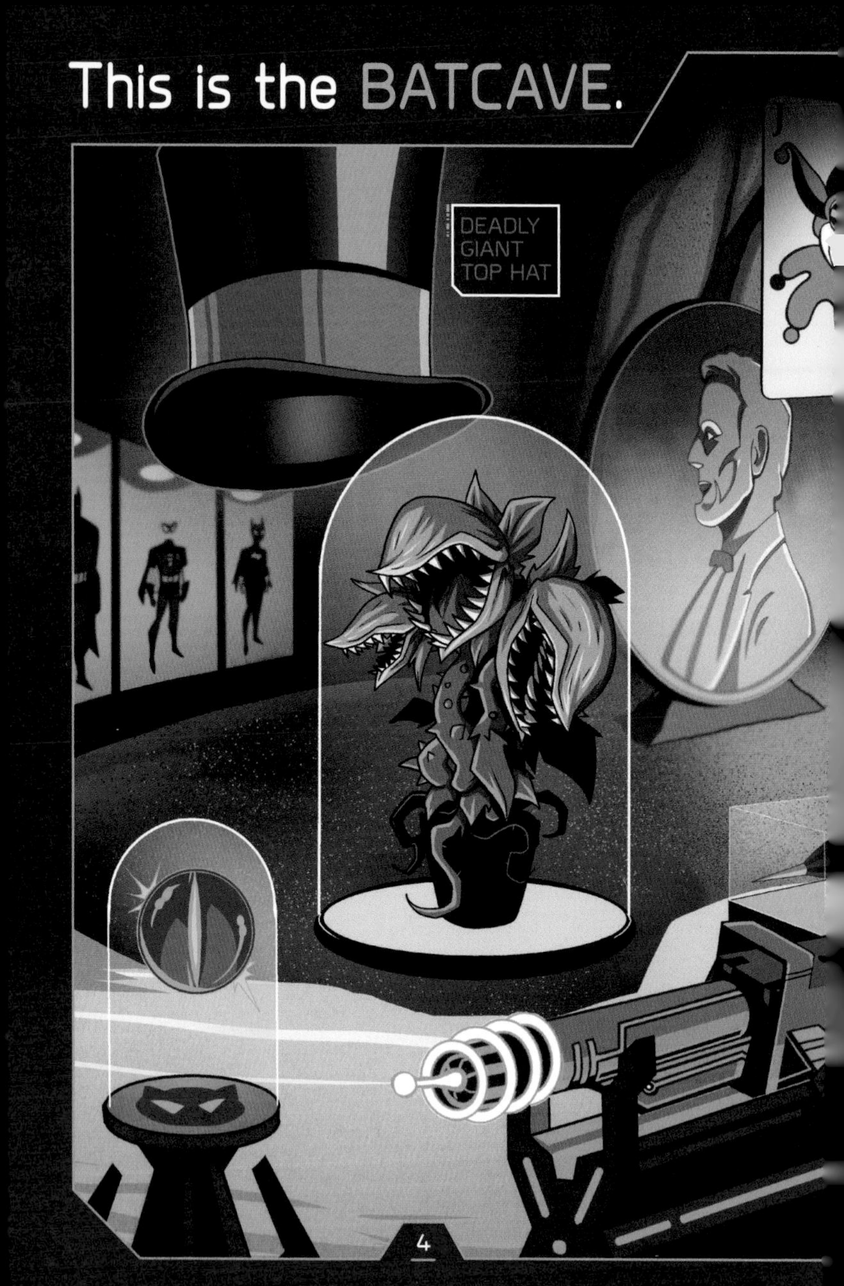
DEADLY
GIANT
TOP HAT

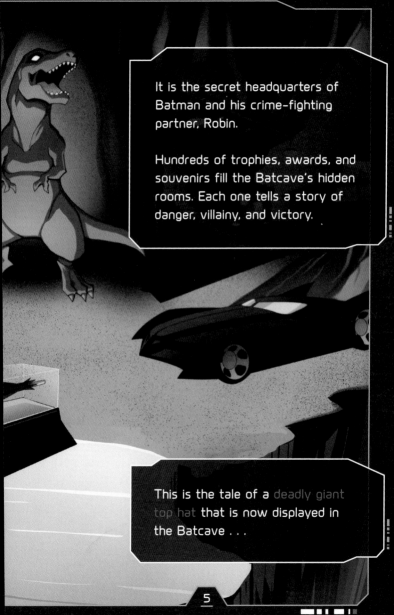

It is the secret headquarters of Batman and his crime-fighting partner, Robin.

Hundreds of trophies, awards, and souvenirs fill the Batcave's hidden rooms. Each one tells a story of danger, villainy, and victory.

This is the tale of a deadly giant top hat that is now displayed in the Batcave . . .

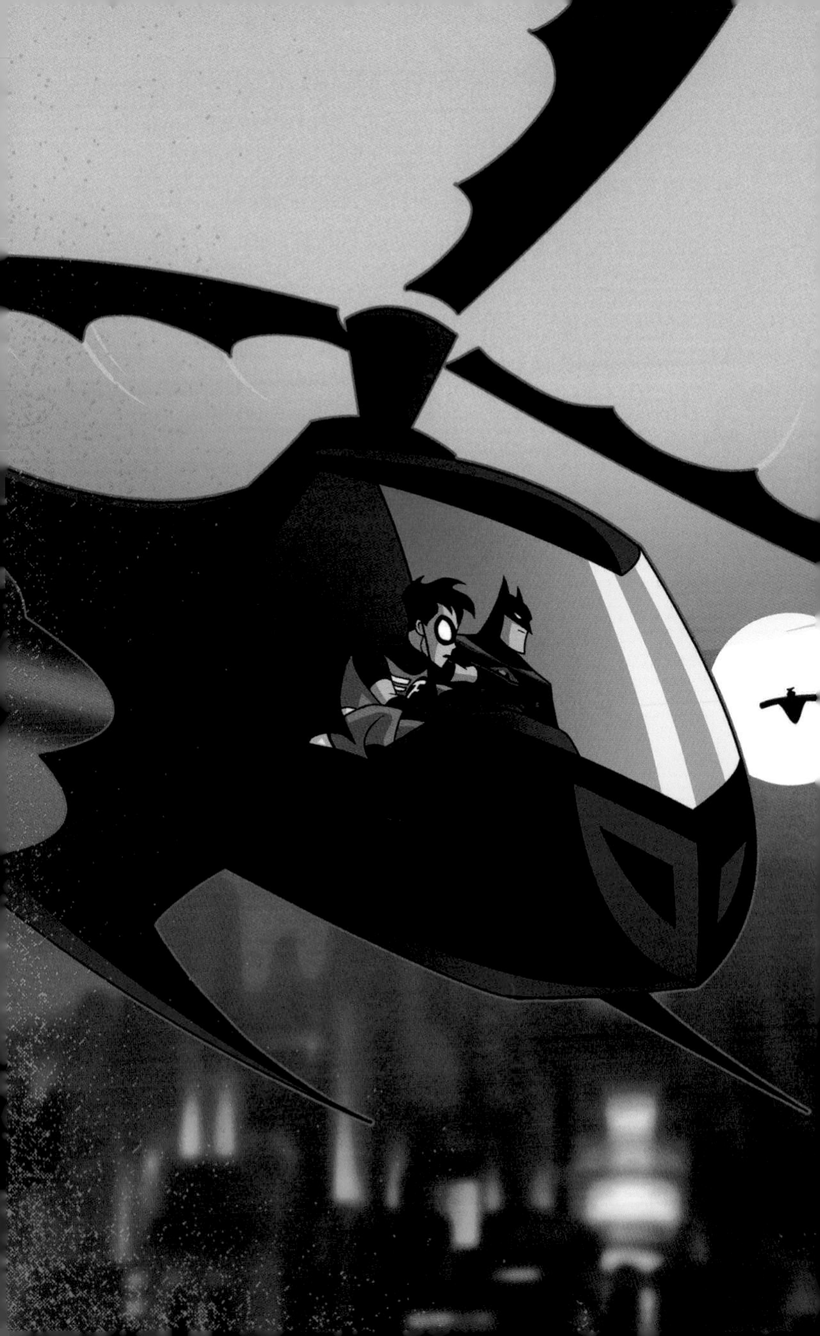

CHAPTER 1

HATS OFF TO HARLEY!

Two strange flying objects race above the gleaming buildings of Gotham City.

WHIRA-WHIRA-WHIRA!

One of the objects is the Batcopter. Inside are the famous crime fighters, Batman and Robin.

"Over there, Batman!" shouts Robin.

They are chasing a giant, soaring sombrero. And sitting at its controls is the dangerous villain, Harley Quinn.

"Give it up, Harley," says Batman.

Harley turns in her seat and laughs at the Caped Crusader.

"I've got hats on the brain these days," she shouts. "Let's see if your brains can handle my straw hats!"

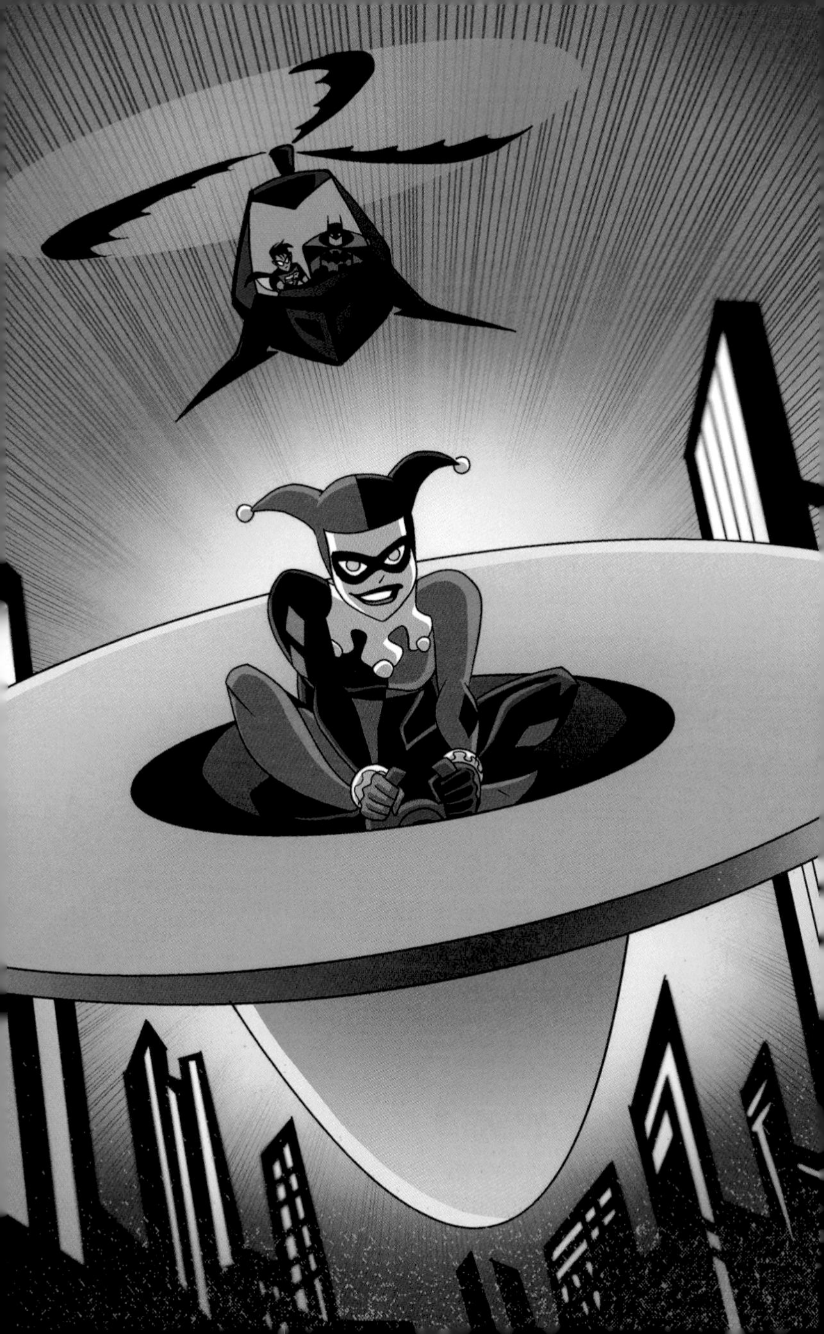

Harley flings several hats into the air behind her. The hats are gold and shiny.

"They're not straw hats. They're SAW hats!" yells Robin.

"Cute, huh?" says Harley Quinn.

BUZZZZ-ZZZZ-ZZZZZ!

The razor-sharp saw hats spin toward the Batcopter.

ZING-G-G! ZING-G-G!

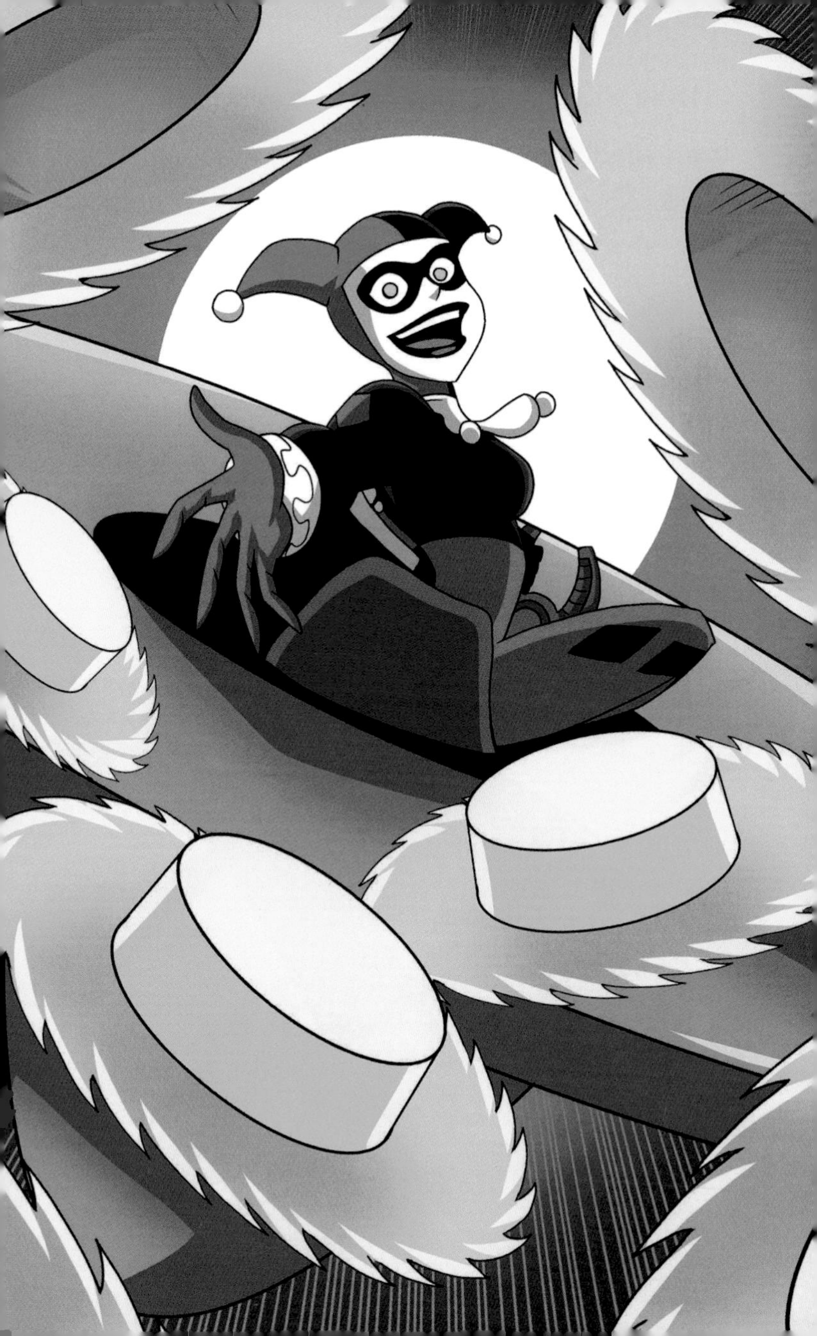

They slice off the tips of the Batcopter's rotor blades. With shorter blades, the copter wobbles off balance.

Batman tumbles from the cockpit.

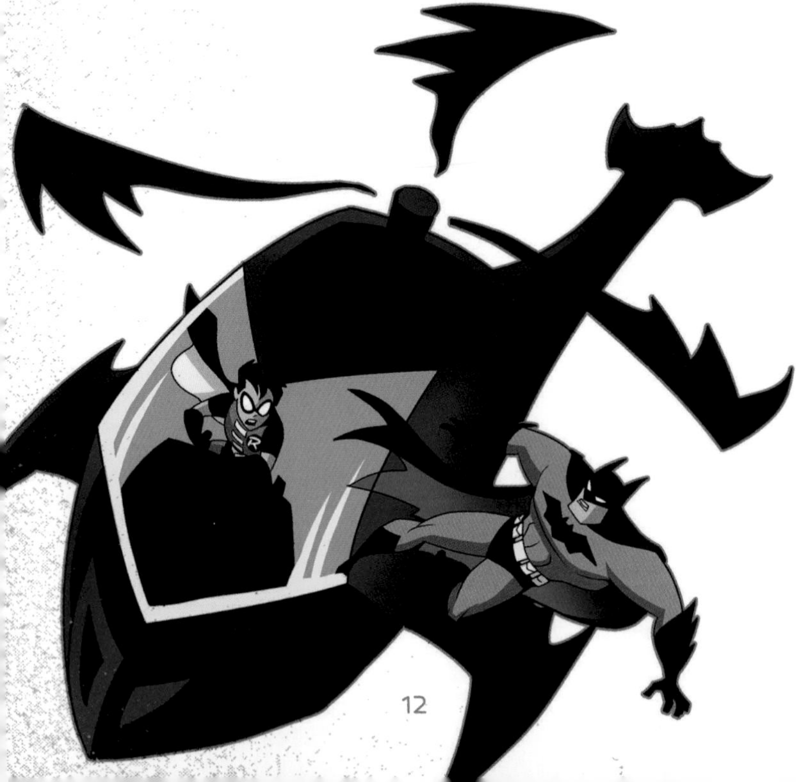

CHAPTER 2

FLYING AND FALLING

Robin leans out and tosses a rope to Batman.

The hero grabs it and swings safely below the Batcopter.

"That's cutting it close," says Batman.

The wobbling copter slows down. Harley Quinn speeds away.

“Hang on, Batman,” says the Boy Wonder.

Robin grabs the control stick and yanks it back.

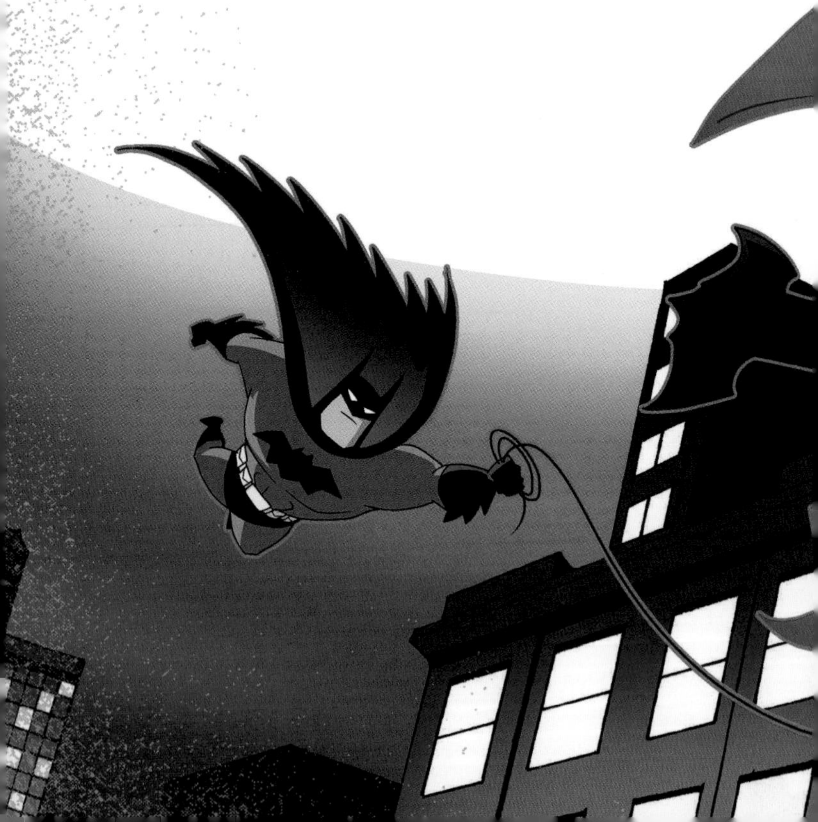

The Batcopter darts sideways between buildings. But its short blades can't handle the weight of two crime fighters for long.

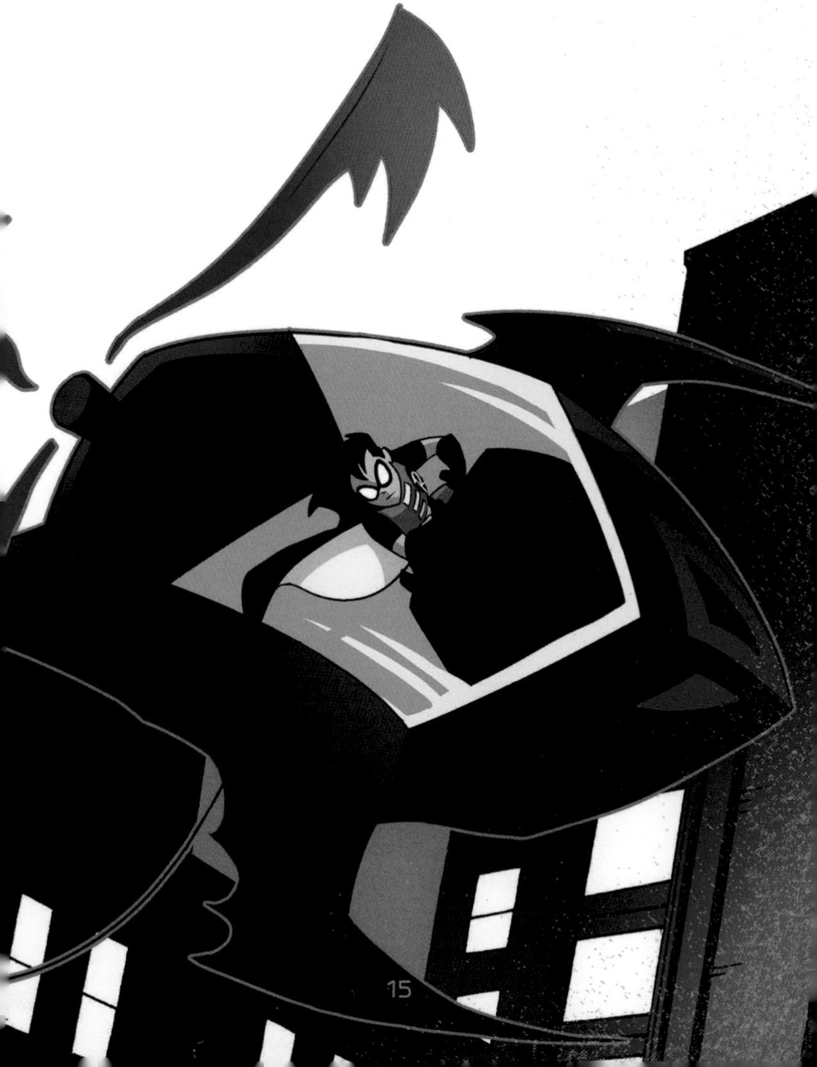

Soon the two heroes see the flying sombrero circling back.

Harley Quinn has another trick up her sleeve.

She picks up a jester's cap. She points the cap's open end at the Dynamic Duo.

"It's *jester* little something I stole this morning," she shouts.

FWOOOOOSHHH!

Strong winds blow from the jester's cap.

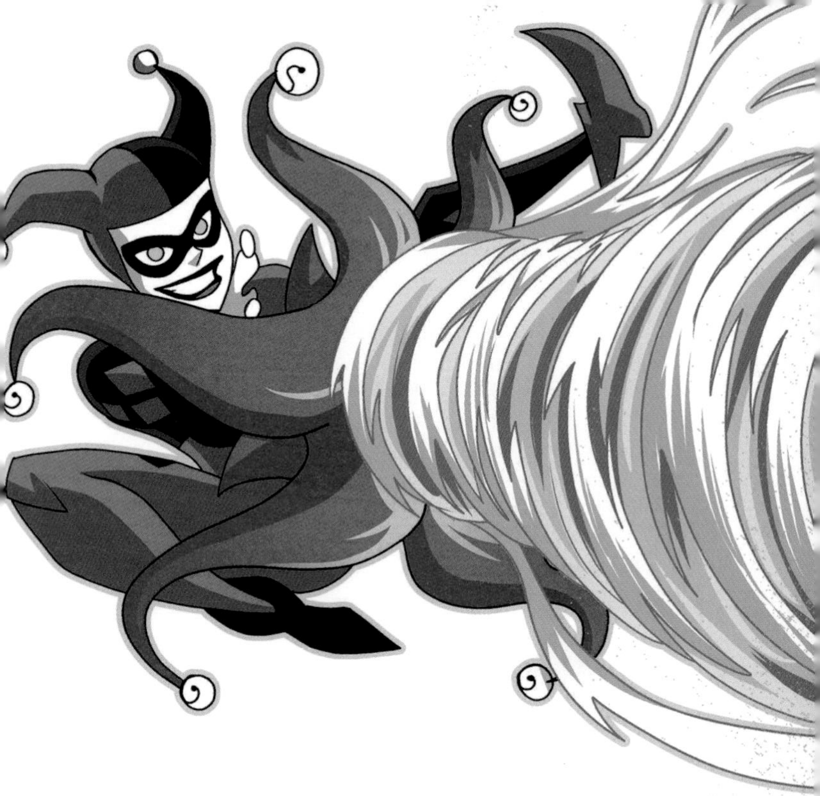

The Batcopter wobbles and shakes. The Dark Knight knows his extra weight is putting Robin in danger.

"Keep after her!" Batman says. He lets go of the rope and leaps toward the buildings below.

"Careful, Caped Crusader," shouts Harley. "Bad stuff can happen at the drop of a hat!"

The Batcopter straightens out. Robin steers away from the stream of wind.

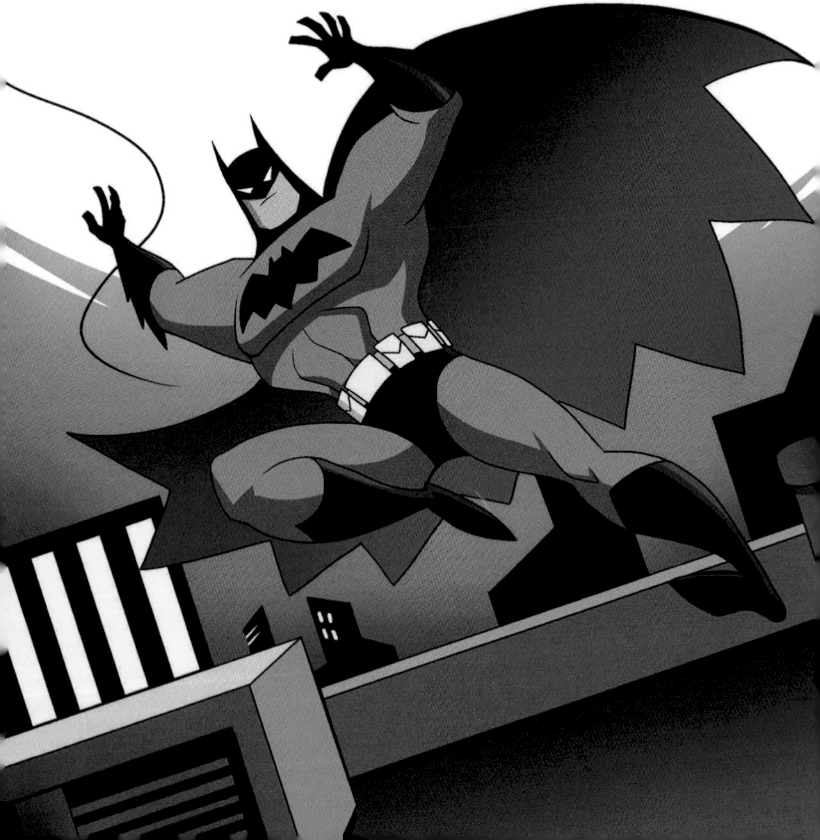

Batman tosses a Batarang toward a nearby flagpole. The weapon's rope wraps around the pole and slows his fall.

The hero lands safely on a rooftop.

While Robin chases Harley Quinn by air, Batman follows them below on foot. He leaps from roof to roof.

Soon Batman sees Harley's sombrero swoop toward an old, empty building.

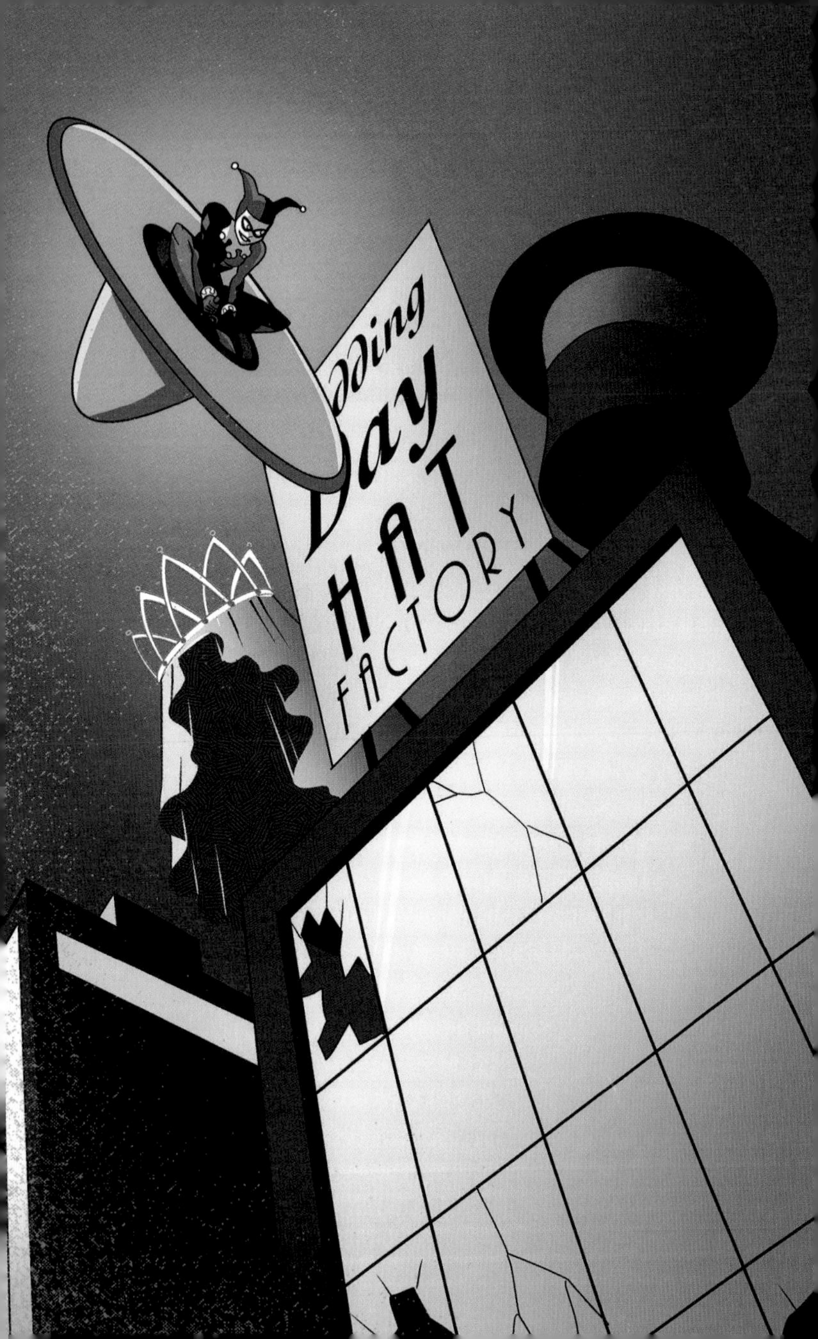
dding
Day
HAT
FACTORY

CHAPTER 3

THE HUMMING HAT

A huge billboard displays the building's old name:

WEDDING DAY HAT FACTORY

Atop the building sits a huge bridal veil and a giant, upside down top hat.

With a leap and a flip, Batman lands on the top hat. He stands and watches Robin flying down to join him.

Suddenly the top hat tilts.

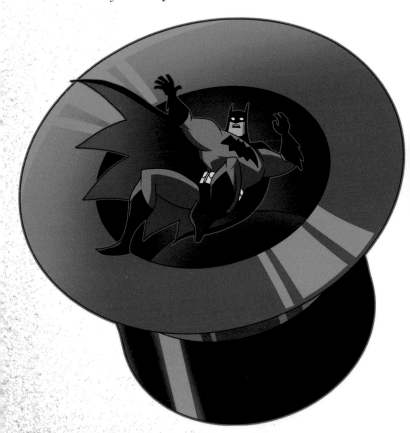

Batman loses his balance and slides into the top hat's giant opening.

The Dark Knight puts his hand against the inside of the hat. It is as smooth as glass.

Harley hovers above the hat in her sombrero.

"You've fallen right into my trap, Caped Crusader," says Harley. She presses a button on a remote control.

HUUUMMMMM!

Batman feels a soft vibration under his boots. He is suddenly pushed against the inside of the hat.

The giant top hat is spinning.

Batman sees his foe flying above the hat.

Harley giggles. "Now I'm off to snare the Boy Wonder. I have a plan that can't *veil* — I mean *fail*!"

The top hat spins faster and faster.

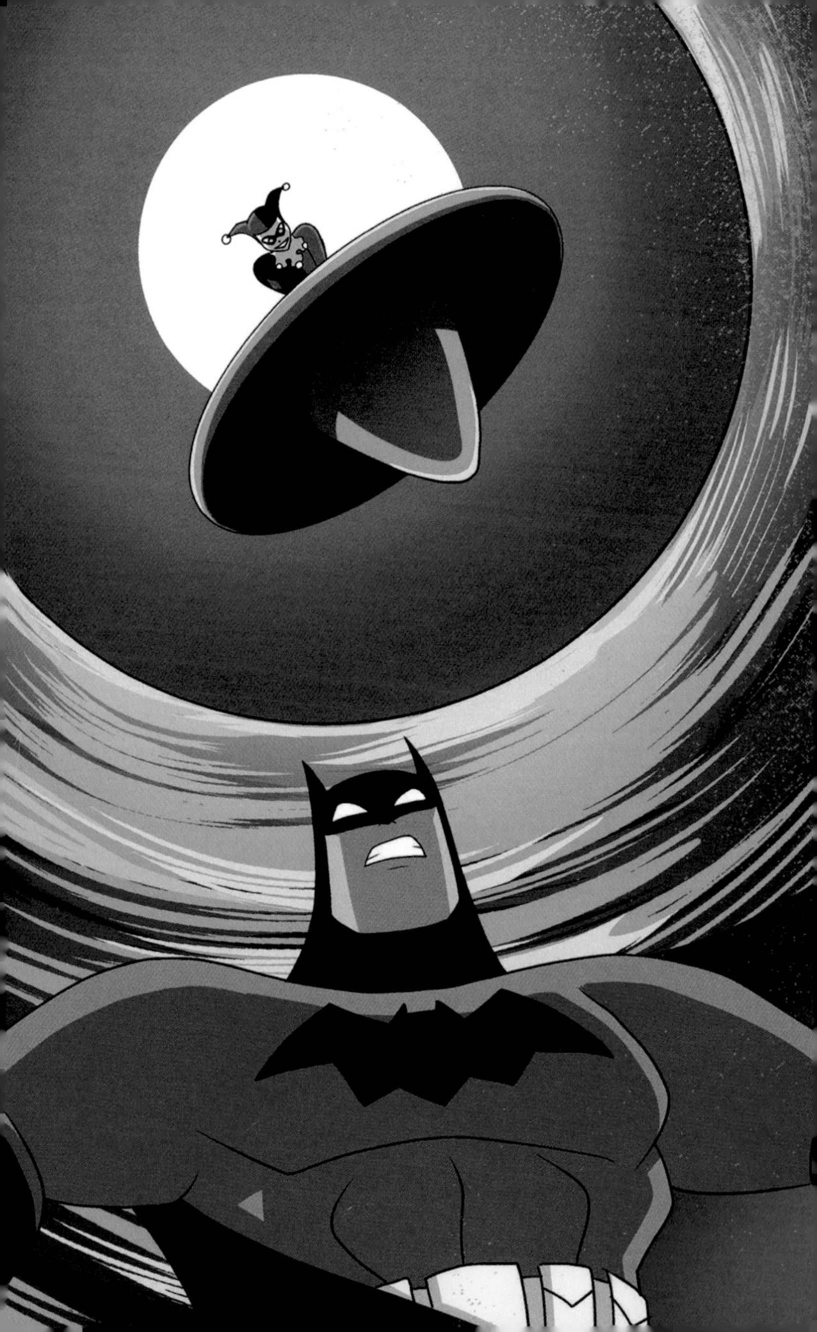

The spinning force crushes Batman against the wall. He knows a Batarang could help him climb out of the hat.

But the force pins his arms flat against the wall. He can't reach his Utility Belt.

Batman presses his palms against the wall. Slowly, he uses his powerful muscles to inch up the side of the hat.

The hat spins faster. It grows harder and harder for him to move.

His head feels dizzy. Batman sees flashing points of light.

He knows this is what people see before they pass out.

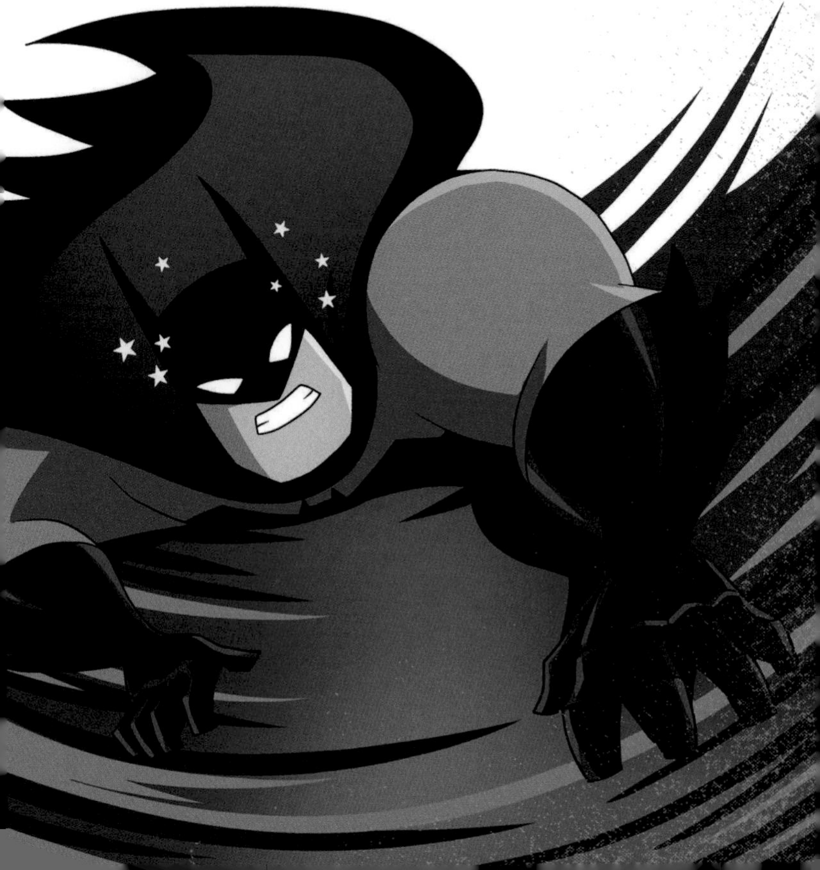

CHAPTER 4

EPIC VEIL

The Batcopter swoops toward the rooftop of Harley Quinn's hideout.

"Where's Batman?" Robin demands.

"Oh the Dark Knight isn't feeling well," says Harley. "I believe he caught something that's going around!"

"But I'm glad you came, Boy Wonder," continues the villain. "You always say that crime doesn't pay. Well then get a load of my *net* worth!"

Harley pushes another button on her remote control. The giant bridal veil begins to expand.

Suddenly the veil springs toward Robin.

The netting grows wider and wider. It hovers above the Batcopter like a dangerous cloud.

It's too big! thinks Robin. *I'll never get away in time!*

CHAPTER 5

WHOSE HAT TRICK?

A glove reaches out of the top hat's opening.

With his last ounce of strength, Batman pulls himself to safety.

The hat is still spinning. Its motion tosses Batman high into the air.

SWOOOSSSHH!

The hero uses his cape to catch the air
like a large kite. Batman coasts down to the
factory rooftop.

"Robin!" he calls. The Dark Knight is worried
about his partner after what Harley had said.

Batman hears the whir of the Batcopter. He
looks up to see Robin aiming the damaged
rotor sideways.

The blades blow the giant veil into Harley
Quinn. The veil wraps her in its sticky mesh.

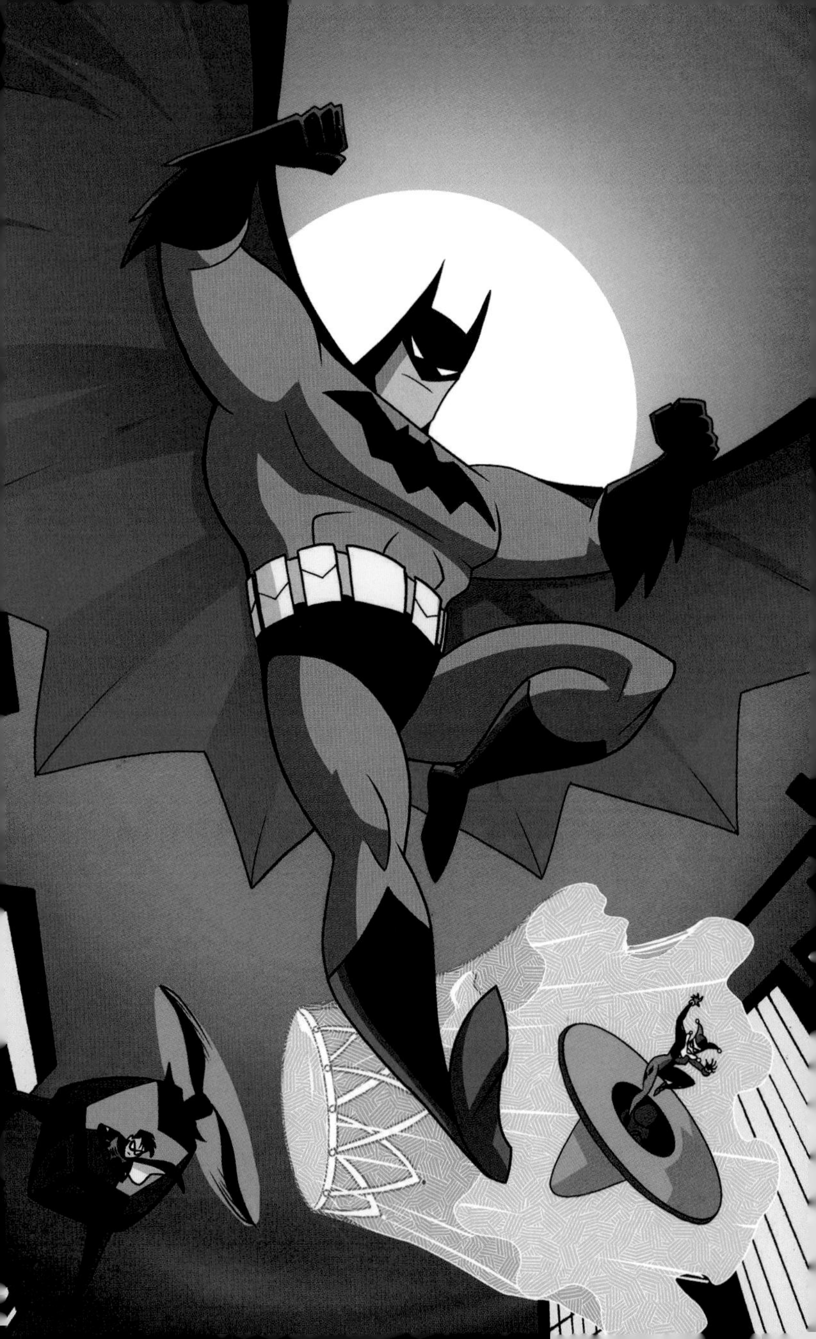

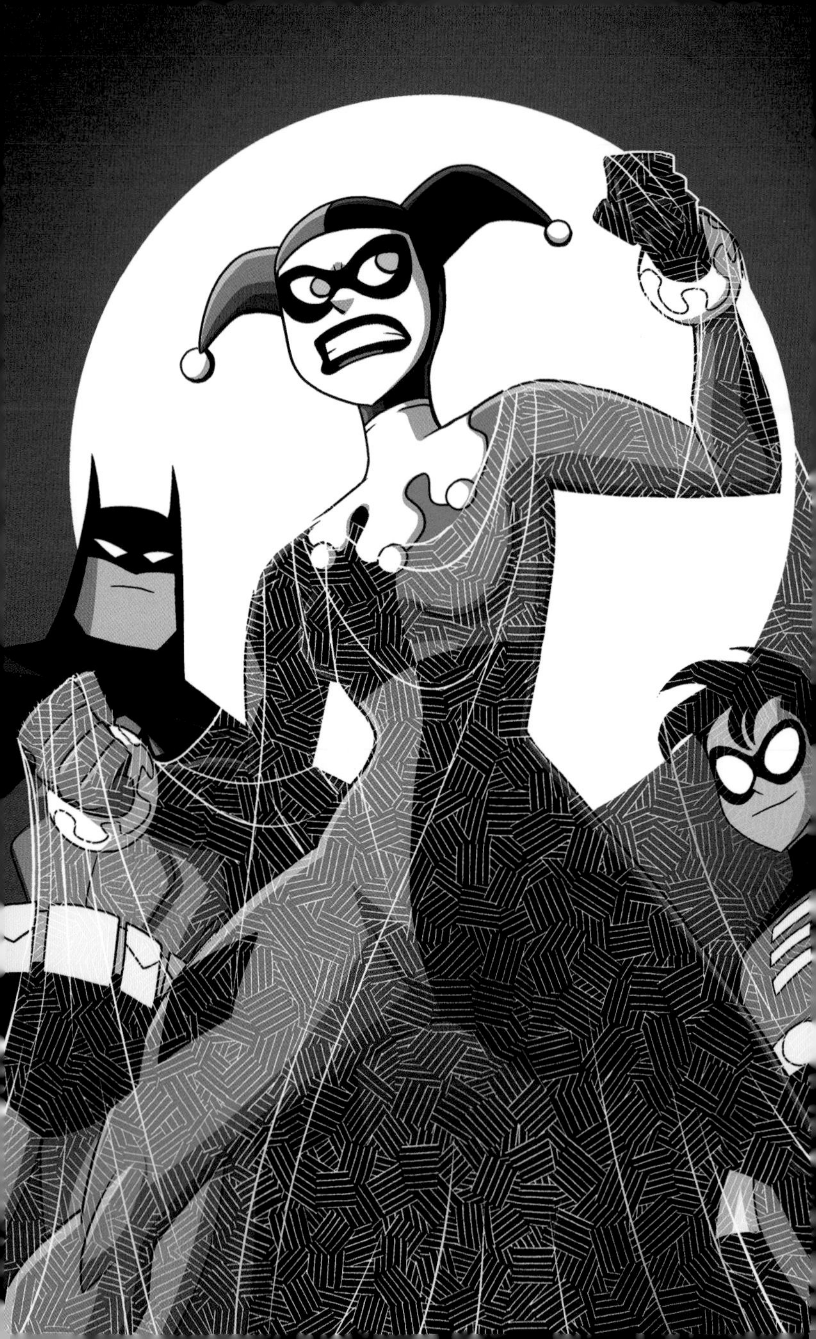

"She thought she'd snare me in this net," says Robin. "But I turned her trick against her."

"Looks like you have everything wrapped up," says Batman. "And you, Harley Quinn, are all out of tricks."

"The Joker is going to hear about this!" shouts Harley.

"The joke's on you, Harley," says Robin. "Next time use your thinking cap before you tangle with the Dynamic Duo!"

EPILOGUE

"Now that we've put a *lid* on Harley, what do we do with this top hat, Batman?"

"Well, it's a shame to leave it here on the roof, Robin."

"Do you think it would look better in the Batcave?"

"What better way to *cap* off the day's adventure?!"

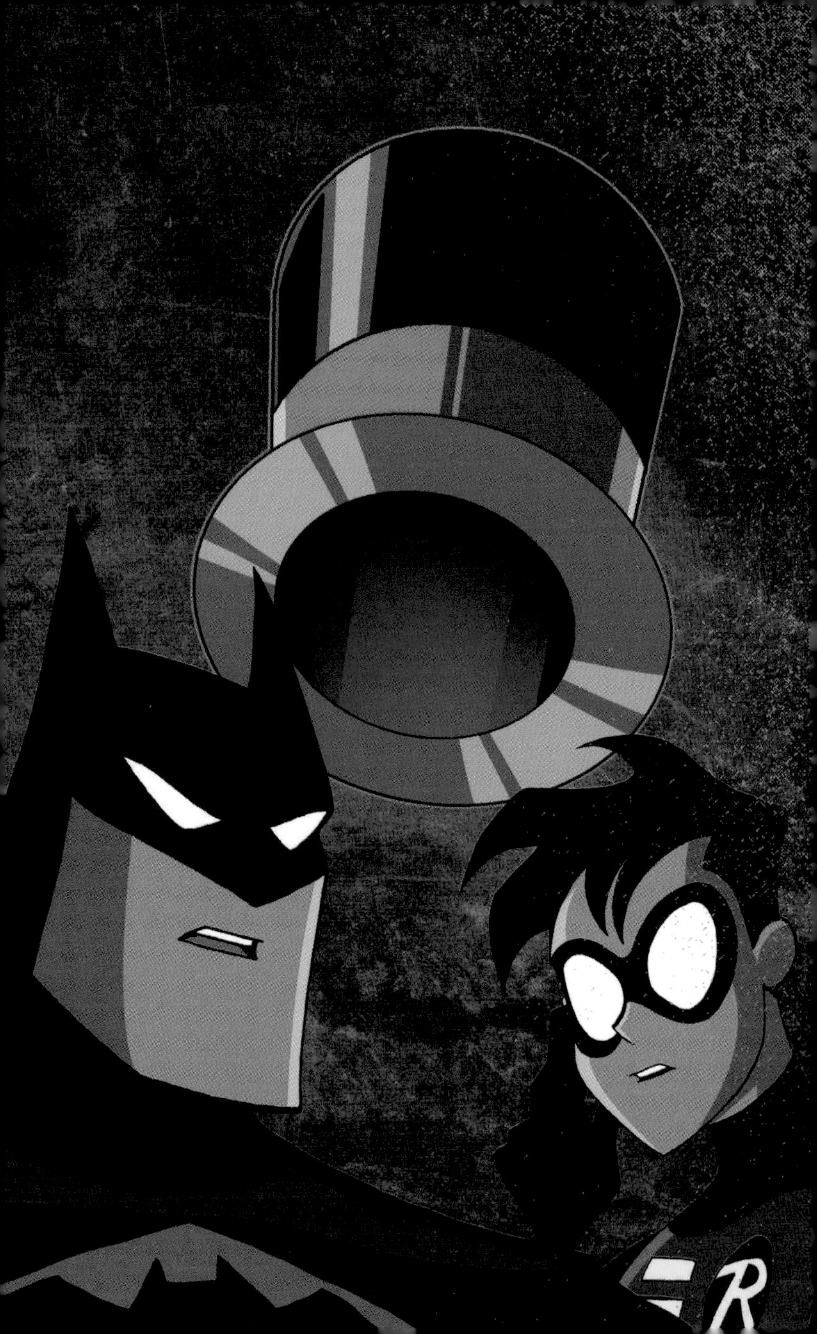

GLOSSARY

bridal veil (BRYE-duhl VAYL)—a covering for the head or face worn by a woman who is getting married

cockpit (KOK-pit)—the area in the front of a plane where the pilot sits

foe (FOH)—an enemy

hover (HUHV-ur)—to remain in one place in the air

jester (JES-tur)—an entertainer at a court in the Middle Ages

mesh (MESH)—a net made of threads or wires

rotor (ROH-tur)—a set of rotating blades that lifts an aircraft off the ground

snare (SNAIR)—to catch or trap something

sombrero (sohm-BRER-oh)—a wide-brimmed hat

vibration (vye-BRAY-shuhn)—a rapid, trembling motion

Discuss

1. Why do you think Harley Quinn uses crazy hats in her caper? What else could she have used?

2. Batman starts to feel dizzy inside the spinning hat. Have you ever felt dizzy or strange inside something that was moving? Discuss what happened.

3. Batman and Robin work well together. Can you remember three examples in the story of their crime-fighting teamwork?

Write

1. Batman was almost defeated inside the spinning hat trap. Was there another way he could have escaped? Think of one, write it down, and describe his actions.

2. Harley Quinn used all types of hat tricks against Batman and Robin. What other hat weapons could she have used? Make a list and describe how they would work.

3. Robin handles the Batcopter with skill in this story. If you had a Batcopter, where would you go? What would you do with it? Write a paragraph describing your adventure.

Author

Michael Dahl is the prolific author of the best-selling *Goodnight Baseball* picture book and more than 200 other books for children and young adults. He has won the AEP Distinguished Achievement Award three times for his nonfiction, a Teachers' Choice Award from *Learning* magazine, and a Seal of Excellence from the Creative Child Awards. He is also the author of the Hocus Pocus Hotel mystery series and the Dragonblood books. Dahl currently lives in Minneapolis, Minnesota.

Illustrator

Luciano Vecchio was born in 1982 and is based in Buenos Aires, Argentina. A freelance artist for many projects at Marvel and DC Comics, his work has been seen in print and online around the world. He has illustrated many DC Super Heroes books for Capstone, and some of his recent comic work includes *Beware the Batman*, *Green Lantern: The Animated Series*, *Young Justice*, *Ultimate Spider-Man*, and his creator owned web-comic, *Sereno*.